YOU ARE **S**PECIAL
YOU ARE **L**♥VED

MELANIE LYNN FOWLER

♥ Melanie

PAPERMOON
PUBLICATIONS
papermoonpublications.com · #imaginationrealized

ISBN- 10: 0-692-85994-2
ISBN-13: 978-0-692-85994-0

Library of Congress Control Number: 2017904100
Paper Moon Publications, Livermore, CA

This is God's love letter to you and me.

A special thank you to Dawn and the Mele family.
I have been shown the sweetest expression
of love and support.

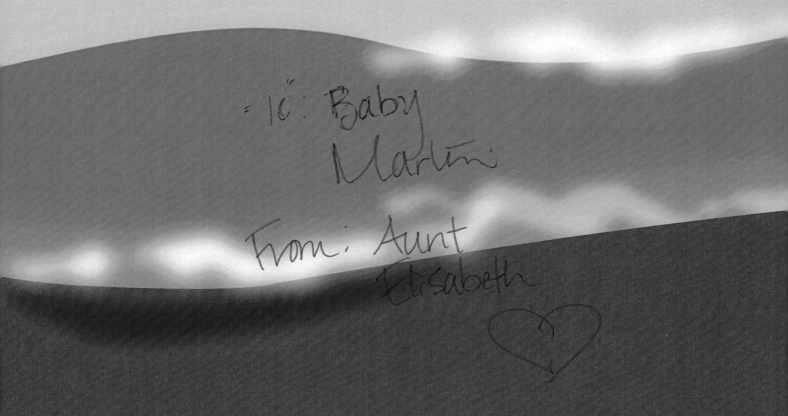

To: Baby
Martin

From: Aunt
Elisabeth

Listen to the little bird,
        such a beautiful sound!

He flies around, ^{up} and down,

through cloud and sky.

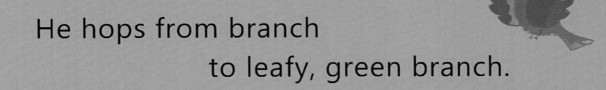

He hops from branch
    to leafy, green branch.

You
are
more
special
than that sweet bird.

Even when your milk is spilled
because you won't sit still,

you are l♡ved.

See the bright butterfly

fluttering,
dancing,
and gliding
from flower
to flower.

She floats on the air
and flies on the wind.

You are more
special than that
beautiful butterfly.

Even when
you forget
to wipe
your feet
at the door,
and mud
gets all over
the floor,

you are so loved.

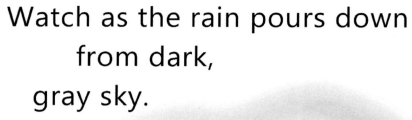

Watch as the rain pours down
from dark,
gray sky.

Drizzle, drizzle
and
pitter-pat.

You are more special
than the glittering rain.

Even when you forget to say,
"Thank you,"
"Please," or
"Please excuse my sneeze,"

you are so very loved.

Feel the playful breeze on your face.

It rustles your hair

and carries away crisp autumn leaves.

It makes
everything swirl.

You are more **special**  than the

dancing breeze.

Even when you have a bad day
or you disobey,

you are so very, very **loved.**

Watch as the sun throws colors
                                    high into the sky.

It goes down behind the hills,

drowsy and slow.

You are

more special

than all the

glowing colors

of the sun.

Even when you don't care
that it would be nicer
to share,

you are so very, very,
very loved.

You are the most special treasure God ever created.

Not a single sparkling star can compare

to how precious you are.

You are so very, very, very,

very loved.

47488330R00020

Made in the USA
San Bernardino, CA
31 March 2017